For Amy, Jo and Jessie, with love—L.G.

For Lisa—C.S.

Craig Smith used ink and Plaka
for the illustrations in this book.

ISBN 0-590-46961-4

12 11 10 9 8 7 6 5 4 3 2 1   6 7 8 9/9 0 1/0

Printed in the U.S.A.   08
First Scholastic printing, April 1996

Where's Mom?

Written by
Libby Gleeson

Illustrated by
Craig Smith

SCHOLASTIC INC.
New York Toronto London Auckland Sydney

On Monday, Dad picked up
Annie, Jess, and baby Jack
from school.

"I think Mom'll beat us home today," he said.

But she didn't.

"Where is she?" said Annie.
"Where's my mom?"
said Jess.
Jack ate some cookies from
the floor.

"I don't know," said Dad.
"What do you think?"

"Maybe she was walking home, and she saw Humpty Dumpty have a great fall."

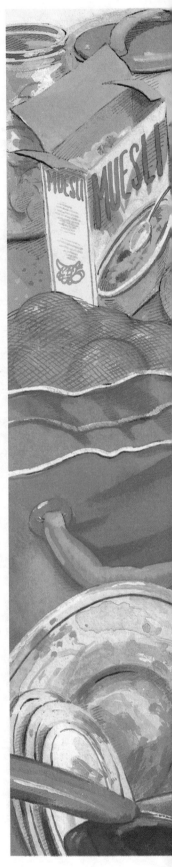

"Or she's gone with Jack and Jill to fetch a pail of water."

"Or she met the three bears, and they've all gone home to have a bowl of porridge."

"I think she met Henny Penny on the way, and she's gone with her to tell the king the sky is falling."

"Or she found the beanstalk, and she's climbed up to the giant's castle to get the hen that lays the golden eggs."

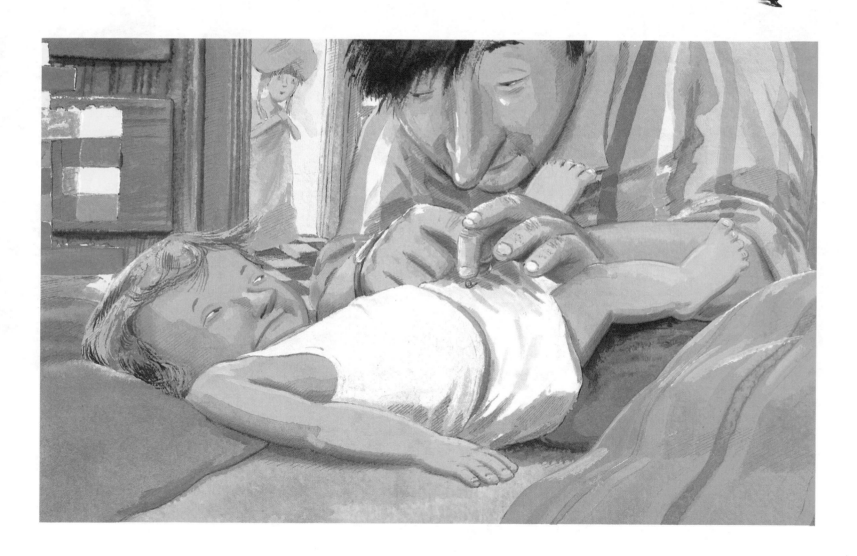

"Maybe she was on the bridge, and the wicked troll wouldn't let her cross."

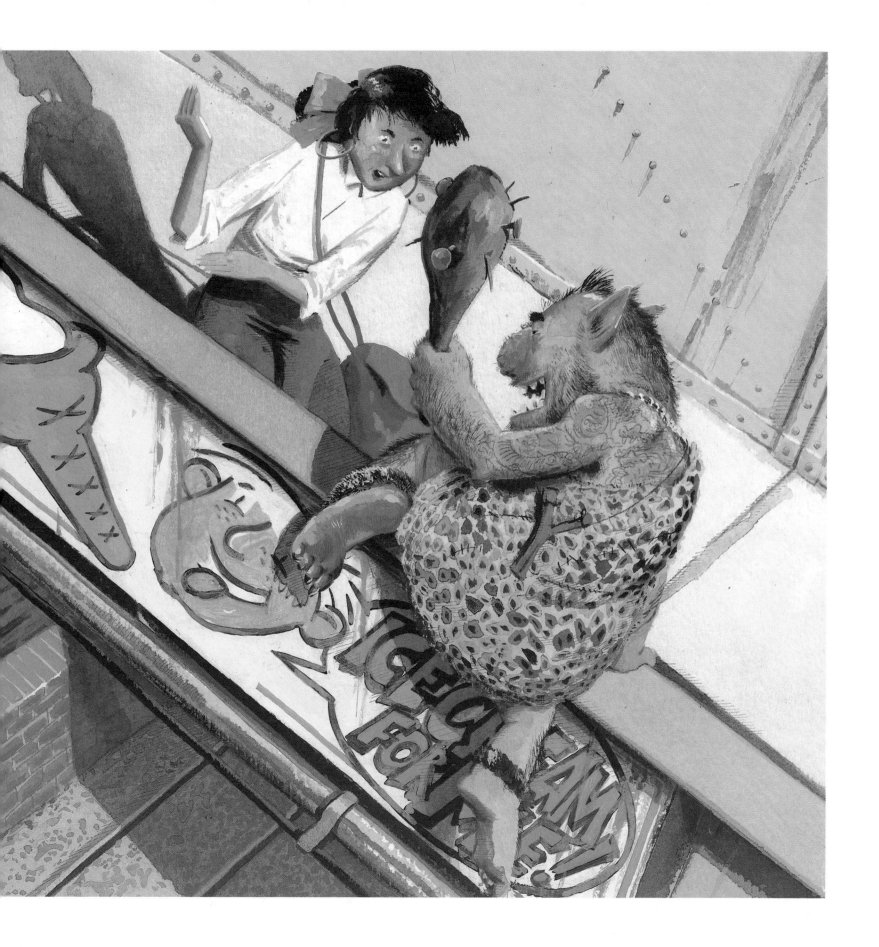

"I know! She was coming home through the dark forest, and she met the big bad wolf, and he tried to gobble her up . . ."

"You'll never guess what happened to me on the way home!"